To
Joseph and Luke,
and Faith and Damien.

Copyright © 2003 by David Lucas
The rights of David Lucas to be identified as the author and illustrator of this work
have been asserted by him in accordance with the Copyright, Designs and Patents Act, 1988.
First published in Great Britain in 2003 by Andersen Press Ltd., 20 Vauxhall Bridge Road,
London SW1V 2SA. Published in Australia by Random House Australia Pty., 20 Alfred Street,
Milsons Point, Sydney, NSW 2061. All rights reserved.
Colour separated in Italy by Fotoriproduzioni Grafiche, Verona.
Printed and bound in Italy by Grafiche AZ, Verona.

10   9   8   7   6   5   4   3   2   1

British Library Cataloguing in Publication Data available.

ISBN 1 84270 218 1

This book has been printed on acid-free paper

Halibut Jackson

by David Lucas

A

Andersen Press
London

Halibut Jackson was *shy*.

Halibut Jackson didn't like to be noticed.

Halibut Jackson liked to blend in to the *background*.

He had a suit that he wore to the *Park*.

He had a suit that he wore to the *shops*.

He had a suit that he wore to the *Library*.

But mostly Halibut Jackson stayed *indoors*.

One day a letter arrived. It was an INVITATION.
An INVITATION on a scroll of silver and gold.
It was an invitation to a *Party*.

*Her Majesty the Queen
would like to invite you to her
Grand Birthday Party.*

*Please come to the Palace
next Saturday.*

RSVP

"The Palace!" said Halibut Jackson.
He had seen *pictures* of the Palace.
How he longed to see the Palace for himself.
The Palace was *silver* and *gold* and covered in *jewels*.

But Halibut Jackson was *shy*.
Halibut Jackson didn't like to be noticed.
Halibut Jackson *certainly* didn't go to parties.
What a shame!

That night he dreamed of the Palace.
He dreamed of *glittering* towers, of *silver* stairs,
of a *golden* door...

And when he woke he had an *idea*.

He began to make a SUIT,
a suit of *silver* and *gold*, covered with *jewels*.

"Now nobody will even notice me,"
said Halibut Jackson.

How was he to know it was a *Garden Party*?

Everybody noticed Halibut Jackson.

And *everybody* wanted a suit like his.
"What a BEAUTIFUL suit!" they said.

"Can you make *me* a suit of SILVER?" said the Queen.
"Can you make *me* a suit of GOLD?" said the King.

"I will do my best..." said Halibut Jackson.

And so Halibut Jackson made a suit for the Queen,
and a suit for the King.
Halibut Jackson made suits for *everybody*.

Before long Halibut Jackson had opened a *shop*,
a shop selling all kinds of clothes,
every kind of suit and hat that he could think of.
In big *gold* letters a sign said: HALIBUT JACKSON.

Now Halibut Jackson had friends.
Now Halibut Jackson had plenty to do.

And although he was still a little shy,
it seemed not to matter so very much at all.